THE FAIRIES' BALL

By Diane Muldrow

Illustrated by Olivia Chin Mueller

For Zara —D.M.

A GOLDEN BOOK • NEW YORK

rhcbooks.com
Educators and librarians, for a variety of teaching tools, visit us at RHTeachersLibrarians.com
Library of Congress Control Number: 2020934951
ISBN 978-0-593-17551-4 (trade) — ISBN 978-0-593-17552-1 (ebook)
Printed in the United States of America
10 9 8 7 6 5 4 3 2 1

Down the path,
over the hill,
into the woods,
then farther still
is a secret place . . .

a mossy ring under the moon's bright light.
This is where fairies will gather tonight!

Flitting and flying, they'll come, one and all,
to the marvelous, magical Midsummer Ball.
Pixies and nixies and brownies and sprites
make merry on this most lively of nights.

Shimmering gowns with silver thread,

blooming crowns on each pretty head—
the fairies have taken months to prepare
their elegant finery, woven with care.

Birdsong and harp, the chirping of crickets . . .
sweet music is heard all through the thickets!

There's sassafras soda for everyone.
The fairies are ready. The ball has begun!

Suddenly, a hush falls over the scene.
A footman announces,
"ALL HAIL THE QUEEN!"

The Fairy Queen leads the dance with a twirl.
The fairies all cheer . . . and the ball is awhirl!

Dancing and chasing by firelight,
the fairies frolic all through the night.

Music and laughter fill the night air . . .

till the queen cries out, "A CAT! BEWARE!"

The terrified fairies cower in fright—
but their brave queen shines
with power and might.

With glittering eyes and a furry scowl,
the cat gives a *hiss* and a long, low growl.

The queen hurls a bolt
of magical light . . .

and she charms the cat
so he won't want to fight!

The fairies laugh when the cat starts to purr.
They flit close to his face and stroke his fur.

Kitty wants to play!
He adds much to the fun . . .

and gives fairies a bed
when dancing is done.